AN EMPTY NEST

SANDY DAY

ISBN-13: 978-1-9990735-0-3

For all the inhabitants of the Beach House.

CONTENTS

ACKNOWLEDGMENTS

My thanks to the Toronto Writers Collective
for the prompt writing workshops where some
of these pieces were first created.

Thanks also to the women who wrote with me
during the summer of 2018,
especially Katie Boyd and Nancy Day.
Without your generous reading and feedback
these stories would not have made their way
into this book.

Thanks to my mom and my sisters
for sharing the space to write and quilt,
summer and winter.

I
STILL LIFE WITH CAT

I'm mid-fifties.

Not the time of bobby socks and poodle skirts. Not the cool Fahrenheit put on a jacket mid-fifties. The age.

I don't even know whether I'm allowed to call myself middle-aged anymore. Whether that's a lie. Whether I'm just plain old now.

I struggle to remember when my mother was mid-fifties and I was mid-twenties. But there's no comparison. She wasn't alone — although I think she often wished she were. My father was alive and driving her up the wall with his drinking and querulous nature, and my sisters and I were always moving out or moving in with various boyfriends, dogs, and cats, before the grandchildren started to arrive.

In contrast, I live an apartment life. There's no house like my mom's, no garden, no savings, no retirement funds, no pension, no husband anymore. Only me and the cats and a perfumed bedroom where my daughter once slept until noon and blared her giant-screen TV while she straightened her hair and smeared foundation onto her flawless skin.

Now it's quiet.

I look around at the mounds of stuff. My stuff. No toys, no husband junk, no children's cast-off sweatshirts. I used to say, don't hang your coat on the floor. Now I say nothing. There's no one here to hear. Only a cat leaving endless fluff drifting into every corner, clinging to the bottom of every chair leg and cupboard. Too much fluff for me to deal with. It's too much. This aloneness. This endless decade blowing by.

2
WHERE'S MY CAR?

Years ago, before I had children, I woke up, or came to, whatever you want to call it — one dry eyelid scraped across an eyeball and I stared into the white freckled flesh of my husband's shoulder. Okay, I was in the right bed. Tick that box. I turned my head and my brain skittered and slammed into the side of my skull. Ouch, that hurt. My other eye creaked open. So now, I was awake. It was light out. Really light, no mistaking it, it was daylight.

I needed more sleep but my bladder squawked, a taut elastic band, and my mouth tasted like a combination of dry corn flakes and moldy lemons. I sat up on the side of the bed. I was wearing one of my husband's t-shirts. My clothes from last night lay in a tangled lump on the floor.

In the bathroom, I stared into the mirror. Under my puffy eyelids, two smears of mascara graced my upper cheeks like two polite black eyes. I guzzled a glass of water then held onto the sink for a moment, waiting for the water to go down into my stomach or come hurling back up.

I walked into the silent living room and looked out the window. Where's my car? I craned my neck so I could see down into the parking lot to the spot next to the walkway, next to the playground, unit 501's designated parking spot.

The bumper and side panel of my car were visible. I felt my breath expel, unaware that I'd been holding it. The car was there. Intact from what I could see. Someone (me?) had driven it home.

I went back to bed. My husband stirred in his sleep as I climbed in. He opened one eye to look at me. Didn't smile. I lay my head on the pillow. My brain sloshed into a new position like fluid in a level.

I'm safe, I told myself. I'm okay. I didn't do anything wrong. I closed my eyes. Then I started to remember.

3
FANCY LICKS

My kids preferred the restaurant called, Licks. And why not? Chicken pieces shaped like dinosaurs and french-fries in a little box with plum sauce, a coupon for a free ice cream cone, and singing fry-chefs while you waited.

My kids loved Licks, they demanded Licks, but I was sick of Licks. And besides I wanted to drink.

So I'd take them to Michelangelo's and tell them it was the *fancy* Licks.

Michelangelo's, an old restaurant. I don't remember when my husband and I first started going there—sometime long before children.

He and I would order dishes like Linguine Pescatore or Penne Arrabbiata, which came with Michelangelo's house salad—a pallid assortment of garden vegetables atop iceberg lettuce with a marvelous dressing that tasted like it was made with the oil from an anchovy can.

The kids wanted garlic bread. Garlic bread with cheese! If we ordered them pasta or anything else, they didn't like it and it just went to waste.

My son, a five-year-old in an Italian restaurant, would order tea. The waiter brought it in a metal teapot on a saucer with a spoon, a china cup, sweeteners, and a bowl of creamers. That was my son's favorite part. The creamers.

Hubby and I ordered a litre of wine to share. Michelangelo's thick red house wine. Robust and tangy, the first glass warmed me and, I imagined, turned my lips an attractive rouge.

I remember waking my mom in the morning when I was a little kid. I'd lean on the side of the bed and look directly into her sleeping face squashed into the pillow. Five years old, the age of my son ordering his tea. I'd ask if she was awake and her eyes would open but she wouldn't raise her head.

"Go back to bed," she'd say and I'd get a whiff of something terrible. A barnyard. A rotten fruit. Her wine breath.

How many mornings did my own children breathe in my poor decisions? I doubt now they were fooled by anything.

They always knew there were no dinosaurs at Michelangelo's.

4

AN EMPTY NEST

A bout of empty-nest syndrome collides with my daughter's urge to get a puppy. Saffron wants *me* to get a puppy that she can come and visit and "help" take care of.

I outline for her the many reasons I will not house a puppy for her. One of them, Ashes, my adult cat that she and her brother had promised to take care of, promised to take with them when they moved out, swore they would love forever, now lives with me in the apartment. Against my will, my children made me a middle-aged cat woman.

Saffron had been the first of my kids to move out. And when my son left to live with my ex-husband, I was sure I was going to relish the solitude. Certain I was going to become productive and tidy and solvent. Life was just beginning after all — the childcare train had left the station, and a husband no longer conducted my life.

So, I am surprised to be slammed by empty-nest syndrome, or more accurately, grief. It wallops me when my messy, smelly, noisy, uncooperative teenage son moves out. I never thought it would happen—I miss him.

I have been alone for several months, with Ashes, when I realize I miss living with another human in the apartment.

Friends ask, what about a roommate? But I've had overnight guests in the now spare bedroom a couple of times and those occasions have shown me that I can't share a bathroom with non-family. I want one of my kids to move home. No, I *need* one of them to move home. But neither Saffron or her brother wants to live with me.

Saffron continues to rattle the cage about me getting a dog. I'm lonely but I want more than canine companionship. We negotiate. Saffron will move back home and we will share a dog, but she will pay for it, and she will take it with her when she eventually moves out.

When Saffron was four-years-old and her brother was one, I'd decided we needed a puppy. I chose a breed that I'd read would be child friendly and I began searching for a breeder. I read all the advice about adopting a dog and had a checklist of conditions a new puppy must meet.

The hunt proved more difficult than I'd imagined but along the way someone told me about a breeder in Peterborough where a friend had got a nice puppy. I called and made an appointment. The breeder had two litters ready to go.

Saffron and I picked up my sister Suze at her farm and headed to Peterborough. Suze was the animal expert in the family—in fact, there was a litter of Jack Russell Terriers in her barn at the time, but all the books said that Jack Russells made terrible family pets.

It was high noon on a hot summer day when we pulled into the Millers Kennels' long dusty driveway. Only the breeder's sign, on a forlorn and crooked roadside mailbox, let us know we were at the right location.

We could hear dogs barking as we got out of the car but bushes screened off the backyard so we couldn't see them.

We knocked at an aluminum door and were ushered into the kitchen of a split-level house. As quick introductions were made, a man in the next room watched a blaring television.

We would see the puppies in the basement—we just had to wait a minute as the woman shouted for her son to help her get organized. We remained in the kitchen eyeing a shelf of hockey trophies and framed school portraits.

After a short time, we were ushered down a circular metal staircase to a basement rec room where the puppies were squirming and crawling over each other in a child's yellow plastic swimming pool.

Instantly, I knew this had been a mistake. The pups weren't eight weeks old, they were much younger. When Saffron knelt excitedly beside the pool, the puppies, afraid and unsocialized, fled to the other side where she couldn't reach them. One pathetic pup, with rusty goop in both eyes and a dry nose, was too lethargic to get away and Saffron's tiny hands were soon picking the puppy up and cradling it to her face.

My mind raced. Certainly, this wasn't ideal, but once safely at home, surely one of these pups would thrive under our care and attention, wouldn't it? We'd driven a long way on a hot summer's day. The price was right and finding a puppy was much harder than I'd realized. Did I really want to begin a new search. But if I said no now, how would I ever get Saffron to put that sickly puppy down?

My sister asked if we could meet the pups' mother. Good idea. The breeder led us out through the back door to the kennels. Immediately, the steady barking turned into a frenzy. Countless dogs were housed in plywood shacks with narrow fenced-in chain-link runs. It was a hot day. Some dogs stood on top of their houses barking ferociously as if they wanted to kill us.

I held Saffron's sweaty little hand tightly as the breeder led us to the kennel of the puppies' mom. She was nowhere to be seen. After a couple of whistles and a sharp call, a cowering female dog slunk from her shack and watched us warily from her platform.

Okay, I'd seen enough. We thanked the breeder and told her we needed to go have lunch and think about it. Saffron chattered at me as I strapped her into her car seat. "When are we getting the puppy, Mom? Which one are we getting? They're so cute, aren't they Mom?" I'd wished I had something to clean her hands.

On the long drive back to my sister's farm, Saffron fell asleep and Suze posed the question, "Why don't you just take one of my puppies?"

Oh no. I'd read horrible things about Jack Russell Terriers. They barked incessantly, destroyed furniture, jumped on everything, and were untrainable, hyperactive maniacs.

A few weeks later, my sister placed a sweet little Jack Russell into Saffron's arms. She grew into a remarkable pet, a wonderful dog, who'd lived to the ripe old age of sixteen years.

Now, years later, Saffron and I are on our way to Port Credit to meet our chosen puppy. Saffron points out the turn-off for Hurontario. She has been anxious the entire drive, worried we won't pass the strenuous list of adoption qualifications the rescue organization has set. I'm not troubled by that. I'm fretting that we might not get Bandit, our first choice, a small black and brown dog that we've chosen from an online profile of adoptable dogs. It's possible there are people in line ahead of us. The rescue has a number of puppies available but from what I read on the website, only Bandit seems suitable for apartment living. What will I do if he isn't available and Saffron sets her heart on one of the consolation puppies, which the website says are a mix of Rhodesian Ridgeback and Labrador Retriever. I don't want a big loud aggressive dog. But if Saffron starts arguing, I won't be able to take her by the hand and lead her away, or strap her into a car seat like I did all those years ago.

I yell at Saffron from the living room where Bandit has chewed another hole in the rug. It's her turn to take him for a walk. I know she's awake—she's been posting pictures of him online. She refuses to come out of her room. She says she's busy right now. She'll take him out in a little while. She doesn't.

Months pass. Bandit grows into a large loud dog. He howls and barks and neighbors complain. The superintendent knocks on my apartment door and issues a warning. Bandit terrorizes Ashes, and I'm afraid he's going to kill her. I spend hours walking him in the howling wind and snow. Then the weather shifts abruptly to stifling heat and rain. Every day, on and on I walk.

Finally, I warn Saffron that I can't look after Bandit on my own and she accuses me of tricking her into moving back home. The day I find another home for Bandit is the day Saffron moves out. Bandit's new owners tuck him into the back seat of their car and drive off down the street. Bandit doesn't glance back at me — he's looking ahead, out the front window, excited to be going for a car ride.

Alone in my apartment, I weep. It hurts as if I've lost everything — and maybe I have. Maybe nothing can replace the family I created and then let go.

5
SIBLING DAY

In April, some sadist invents a new holiday called Sibling Day. Friends on Facebook post photographs of their brothers and sisters lined up in rows, Polaroids and black and whites, the old days, affection and attention.

My sisters remain silent, and I don't possess any pictures to post. I know there is one, somewhere, of the three of us — Natalie, Suze and I lined up with Mom and Dad — but I don't have a copy. Besides, I am painfully aware that there wasn't much sibling love in that photo, or in our lives. My sisters were close in age but I was an alien, born several years after they were. My father thought it was funny to suggest that I was adopted, as though he doubted my paternity. Then he'd say that when I was born I looked like an ancient old relative by the name Effy Smellie. That was her actual name.

My sisters didn't warm up to me though I revered them and tried to tag along. Suze was often downright cruel and unless she needed me for something Natalie ignored me. Until I was older and noticed other people's families, sibling closeness was something I didn't know existed. There was no cheery closeness among us. No loving strokes or tender murmurs. No hugs. No sisterly cuddles.   No love. Our parents didn't model love — I never once saw them kiss — so my sisters and I didn't learn to love, at least not by showing affection.

One time, possibly the same year the missing photo was taken — I was swimming in the lake with my cousin, Hannah. My sister Natalie was playing lifeguard — standing on the end of the dock in her flip-flops and skirted two-piece bathing suit, with a whistle hanging around her neck. Hannah and I were up to our armpits in water, our bare feet sliding around on the slimy stones on the bottom of the lake. We would have preferred to swim farther out at the sandbar but Natalie insisted we play lifeguard or swimming lessons or some bossy game of her choosing.

Natalie had a hard, round, life-saving ring tied to the end of a long yellow rope. She was swinging it back and forth, preparing to launch it toward us and then haul us back to the dock through the water.

It was a breezy summer day. The wind was blowing sideways and the lake was choppy. A seagull flew over caw-cawing. Maybe I was looking at the seagull. Or maybe I was looking through the water, scanning the bottom of the lake for those horrible green leeches that sometimes adhered to the stones. But whatever I was doing I didn't see the heavy, round, life-saving ring sailing through the air toward me.

Thwump.

My cousin Hannah must have saved me. She must have pulled me up and out of the water and towed me to the dock.

I don't remember that part. All I remember is waking up on my towel on the lawn with a box of pink Elephant Popcorn beside me. I remember wondering if I'd fallen asleep in the sun, and where the popcorn had come from. I remember wondering why Natalie was being so nice to me.

Scrolling through Facebook on Sibling Day is like looking at exhibits in the zoo — intriguing, amusing, but foreign and somewhat preposterous.

And then I start to cry and I cannot stop.

6
CASTOFFS

I begin clearing out my bedroom. I'm moving into the family cottage for the summer with my sisters. It was my mother's idea. Natalie, a retired schoolteacher, has spent all her summers at the cottage forever and ever, and Suze works part-time selling fish at the local grocery store. I haven't quite figured out what I will do for work but I'm making enough money freelancing to get by for a few months. In the fall, when the cottage becomes too cold to inhabit, I will move with Suze into my mom's house in the town nearby. Yes, I'm mid-fifties and I'm moving back home.

I sort my clothing into stacks. First, dirty laundry, which consists of assorted pillowcases, t-shirts, and leggings that I find scrunched in a layer of fur and grainy dry cat vomit under my bed. In a second pile, clean clothes that I want to keep. In a third enormous and final pile, years and years' worth of clothes that are too tight or too loose or I don't like anymore. I stuff the latter into plastic garbage bags for the drop box.

The waste nags at me — a mountain of North American old clothes must be accumulating somewhere. The other day on the internet I saw a little kid from Africa wearing a rock 'n' roll concert t-shirt. The excess of first-world living is rampant.

When she comes to see how the packing is going, Natalie tries to reassure me. "It's all recycled now," she explains with authority. "They shred the old stuff and reconstitute it into something else. It all gets used." I'm dubious but Natalie does know a lot about fabric. She's a quilter. No snippet of fabric is too small for her to salvage.

Over the next few days, I drag bags of old clothes and linens down to the elevator and out to the charity bin behind the apartment building.

More troubling, and less convenient, I have to find a home for my cat, Ashes. Natalie is allergic and my mom doesn't want any pets.

I whisper to Ashes curled up asleep on my bed, "This is our last night together." She opens one green slit of an eye. "Tomorrow you'll be with new people." Ashes closes her eye and sleeps on. "They will love you." I feel a lump rising from my chest into my throat. "You'll be fine," I console the sleeping cat. And this part I whisper really low, "And I love you, don't ever doubt that."

The next day, it's tricky to catch Ashes and trap her in the carrying case. She tries to dart past me to the safety of the shoes at the base of the coat rack but she isn't quick enough and within a moment, I'm lifting Ashes by the scruff of her neck and lowering her into the open carrier. A puddle of pee pools on the floor. Ashes yowls.

I set the cat carrier on the back seat of the car. It's only a short distance to the address Jenna from Kijiji gave me. I don't say anything to Ashes about how destitute the housing looks—a low row of ugly apartment buildings. Through the gloom and naked trees, I locate the driveway and park at the rear entrance. Jenna from Kijiji greets me and with only a glance, we glean enough information about each other to proceed with the transaction— one stranger placing a beloved pet into the custody of another stranger.

A voice in the back of my mind whispers, "What the fuck are you doing?" but I ignore it. I also whisper nothing further to Ashes. All the ear scritching and whisker rubbing is done.

In Jenna from Kijiji's tiny basement apartment, Ashes flees from the opened carrier and disappears behind a mattress leaning against the wall. Ashes doesn't look back. She doesn't whisper, goodbye. She is gone and I drive back to an empty apartment to finish packing.

7
PRIMAL LANDSCAPE

It feels as if the key is about to break off in the lock. I struggle to turn it. Is it to the left, or the right? I can't remember. The lock gives way suddenly and the door swings open. Inside, the cottage smells like a birch-bark box. And the air is snappy. Cold. Locked inside for the entire winter it stirs around me, slipping past, through the screen door, a small sigh, a held breath, a secret.

The porch furniture is crammed into the living room. We will pull it outside later. Every year we vow to power-wash the white wicker and give it a fresh coat of paint, but every year it remains on the porch, chipping and greying, the crevices filling with the grime of living.

I walk down the cavernous hallway. Aunt Madge's oriental runner under my shoes feels like millennia, a familiar wrinkle, a soft crush.

At the utility panel in the corner of the bathroom, I throw the electricity switch up and push in the lever that will start the hot water tank twitching and creaking.

My bedroom is a vault, dim, even in the

morning light, the pine tree outside the window shades the light. Leaving the overhead light off, I set my suitcase on the bed.

In contrast with the cool grey of the rest of the cottage, the kitchen glows with a soft golden light. Natalie is emptying a grocery bag of vital supplies, an enormous box of Yorkshire Gold tea and a bag of milk. "There!" she says as if she's accomplished an enormous task.

I feel unhinged and restless. I don't know how I'm going to live with my sisters, if I'll be able to hold my own, or stay in one piece. I don't know how to make this place my home, though I've been coming here all my life.

Unpacking, I take out the crystals. I'm going to hang the angel over the front door—she's stained glass, made by a friend, she'll welcome in the good spirits—and a heart prism, given to me by another friend on my fiftieth birthday, is going over the back door. When the lake is rough and roaring, this hallway is a wind tunnel. In the morning, there's often a biting little breeze from the east, from the sunrise, which sneaks in the back door and thwarts the chill from lifting inside the cottage even on a summer day. This yawning hallway worries me. It feels as if the air between the two doors runs unimpeded and all the blessings I'm trying to lay down will be swept out in a draft. At least the crystals will catch the spirits and give them a swirl before allowing them to pass through the doors.

I'm placing shrines in all the rooms—some element of earth, air, fire, and water in each. My grandmother's cowry shell is going in the living room because I want to tell our kids how we used to play a game with it called Huckle Buckle. The kids are grown now—all in their twenties and thirties—but still I have this desire to impart a piece of our collective past. My sisters and I grew past our teenage years, and for a short period, we'd bonded. I want to tell them about that uproarious time—a time of hilarity and revelry. The years before we fell to one form or another of the family curse and disintegrated.

8
CROWS

Some mornings the crows are so noisy they wake up the entire shoreline. My mom said that one day last week, she looked out to see what all the ruckus was about and saw a skittish red fox slinking across her backyard. The crows gang up on such intruders. Sometimes an owl sets them off. They screech and cry and harangue until the danger passes before finally shutting up.

Seventeen years ago, my father died of throat cancer. It was this time of year. After he died, I noticed the crows were unusually conspicuous. One in particular hung out in the spruce tree near the kitchen window cawing its persistent and irritating caw.

"That's Dad," I told my mom. She didn't disagree.

When my dad was young, he had shiny black hair, slicked back with Brylcreem. He was agile and slim. He had a devilish grin and he laughed quietly from his chest, a pipe clamped between his stained teeth, a master of self-control.

Dad's ashes came from the undertaker in a box about the size of a shoebox. My mom decided we would scatter them on the third hole of the golf course.

We walked out, late one afternoon, my mom, Suze, Natalie, and I, our husbands and children, a few of my dad's old cronies, and Raymond, our cousin who had wound up with the golf course from our great-great grandfather's estate. Dad had loved golfing. When he'd married my mom, they were given a lifetime membership to the golf course, and over his seventy years, he'd played a couple of rounds, every weekend, of every summer. Even when he went blind.

The third hole is way out in the woods surrounded by towering pines — a dead-end alley that as you approach is like walking into a cathedral of trees. The crows were there before us cawing and caw-cawing from the nether regions of the pines.

My cousin Raymond was the first to speak. He eulogized Dad fondly, Uncle Artie he called him, and when he was finished, he wondered, was there anyone else who wanted to say a few words?

In the preceding days, I had practiced reading Dylan Thomas' "Do Not Go Gentle into that Good Night" out loud. But I couldn't get through the whole piece without my throat clenching and the tears starting—and besides, it felt untrue. Dad *had* railed against the dying of the light. He had battled with the thief who'd stolen his voice, his saliva glands, and his wicked tongue. We'd all wondered—why is he fighting so hard? None of us could imagine what he thought he had to live for. He couldn't see, he couldn't swallow, and he couldn't even walk anymore. He'd become more than a nuisance—he was a burden, that at the end, we were relieved to shed.

Those words are so harsh. But my feelings for him are cold stones, stashed away, deposits like gallstones, built up over the years from deficiencies in his affection and attention and love.

Mom brought spoons and the kids dug into the crunchy ashes. There was a lot to scatter, five pounds of gravel. The crow chorus began as we sprinkled my father's bones and teeth around the third green. They cawed and flapped to higher branches as his eyeballs and testicles were poured into the hole, flung into the surrounding bushes, and finally dumped into the soft layers of pine needles.

When all the ashes were gone, we walked back down the fairway. Leaving the crows in the cathedral, protesting or laughing, I couldn't tell which.

9
COTTAGE COUNTRY

It's been a stormy June — it probably broke some record for rainfall. The farmer at Apple Acres tells us about the blotches on his apples, about the tasteless strawberries, and the short corn. He says these sudden showers of heavy rain don't penetrate the ground — when he dug up the garlic, the earth was hard and dry.

Thunder rumbles in the distance, daily, hourly. Abruptly, the rain comes crashing down for a few minutes. Thunder reverberates continuously across the big lake and we see clouds darken and move east or west — yesterday it was south.

My cousin Hannah takes the kayak out and slithers down the bay, looking at the big new houses with shiny windows springing up along the shore. The boomers are renovating old family cottages she reports.

The Ash trees are dying. It's a slow death. I see a squirrel's nest in one, a tangle of orange brown leaves crammed into a crook at a dizzying height.

The renters at the cottage next door are

going home today. Packing up their apricot poodle and their inflatable cocktail lounge and decamping for the city. New renters will arrive and it will take days to get used to them.

No wood ducks in the trees this morning. Just the wind in the branches, and the blue jays jeering. Thunder—and the sound of summer cottages waking, screen-doors slamming. I smell coffee brewing. I don't care if it rains.

10
TOM'S LAST SUMMER

Through the grass, Tom trots toward me, silently over the worn path as though to greet me, but when I bend down to touch his head he dekes out of my reach. No way is he going to let me pat him.

As thin and rickety as an ancient old rocker, Tom's dark coat is rough and rumpled. Obviously, he no longer spends any of his precious energy on grooming. I notice the fur on his stomach is dripping. He's been in the lake. Probably hunting goslings along the shore. The other day behind the cottage, I almost stepped on a decapitated gosling head — downy, a glorious brown and yellow like a tiger, yellow beak sticking out the front like a candy-corn. Only Tom knows what happened to the rest of the gosling's body.

I remember Tom as a kitten — an adorable striped tabby in a litter of patchy white mongrels. I was allowing my children to choose a kitten from the litter. I held back from pointing out Tom's superior black markings. He was a replica of a cat I'd owned at age nine,

Tigger, and a cat I'd owned at twenty-nine, Murray.

Saffron had chosen Tom's pink padded littermate, Mr. Whiskers, as she called him, mostly white, but with uneven blotches of tabby stripe on his back and face. An overly friendly cat, he was a meticulous groomer who kept his white fur gleaming. He roughhoused with our Jack Russell and when you picked him up—he wrapped both paws around your neck and hugged you.

My cousin Hannah took Tom.

Nearly twenty years later, Tom is making the most of his final days. He's on medication, his thyroid under functioning but that doesn't stop him from running down to the beach when the setting sun attracts a crowd of watchers, or from hunting small creatures. I saw him running across the lawn the other day with a limp chipmunk dangling from his mouth.

Mr. Whiskers had lived only a short time. My ex-husband had taken him when he'd moved into a small bachelor pad on Kingston Road. He'd allowed the cat to roam, unwilling to stay cooped up in a dingy hot apartment with a frisky young cat. Mr. Whiskers died on a side street, run over by a parking car.

I admire Tom. I admire the way he's throwing his weight around, even if he has no heft to speak of. I look into his ancient old eyes, the irises scaly and reptilian, but only for a moment before he looks away, trotting off into the cedar hedge, through the ferns to the neighboring cottage. No time to chat. No time for petting. He's on a mission. It's his last summer but this deathwatch is no sorry state.

II
VENOM

I struggle with generalities—my mind latches hard onto fiction, friction, gossip. Words of wisdom slip by me, forgotten, misremembered, but stories sink deep—like fangs into my arm spreading venom.

I watch crime shows in my bed at night. I'm addicted to a morbid stream of murders and treachery, heroes and villains. And I'm picky about my crime—discarding plots that don't immediately ensnare me. I'm aware of the paradox. My placid, law-abiding existence, butting up against blasting gunshots and sheeted corpses. Violence flickers across my screen as I gobble cookies and sip tea. Brilliant detectives know just what to say and just who to trust. I go to sleep sated with criminality and retribution, lawlessness and justice, I sleep and dream of old boyfriends and vengeance.

12
EVICTION

We have an old pump house in our lane. My grandmother once told me it's sitting on top of a one-hundred-and-fifty-foot artesian well. But we're on town water now.

The birdhouse nailed to the side of the pump house was Grandpa's doing. He loved his wild birds.

A person could easily reach up, lift the lid of the birdhouse, and disrupt the nest inside but the birds don't seem to consider that. A sparrow has claimed it this year, an ordinary drab sparrow whose nestlings cry and chirp pitifully each time she appears at the hole.

Inside the old pump house, an animal has been eating our garbage. A few days ago, I unlocked the door and found the contents of a black plastic bag strewn all over the floor and lawn mower.

I come home late one night. The car-lights sweep down the driveway, a tunnel of cedar hedge and thick leaves. A shape slinks across the drive — black and white. The skunk, paying no attention to the car, shuffles in front of me. Then from the thick grass beside the pump house, another skunk emerges, squeezing its furry body from the gap I now see between the ground and the bottom boards.

The garbage eaters disappear into the dark hedge.

I wait, frozen. Windows rolled up. I park and exit the car as soundlessly as possible. I run to the cottage, sniffing the air in apprehension.

No skunk.

The next day I sweep up the garbage from the floor of the pump house, hoist the bag into a trash can, and place a brick on the top.

The birdhouse is quiet. The sparrows have moved out, or they're asleep. I'm not going to open the lid to find out.

13
MOUSETRAP

A mouse in the attic is rolling golf balls. The sound wakes me and I wonder how a mouse got golf balls way up into the ceiling. I picture Samuel Whiskers and the Roly Poly Pudding although it's possible that this mouse is slender and small and not a rotund rat in a waistcoat.

Every fall, before we leave for the winter, we put down poison. Little china dishes of strychnine-laced mouse seeds. At first, the mice probably think it's nice of us to leave them a little feast for the winter. In the spring, the seed is always gone, and there is scant sign of mice. Just a few miniature poops in the warming oven, and some droppings on the shelf in my closet, under a duvet and pillows. Not like the year when a mouse unraveled the corner of a beloved hooked rug.

Now, a mouse is rolling golf balls in the attic. It's not creepy scampering across the ceiling—it's loud and unmistakable. And a mouse has been spotted, on more than one occasion, like the shadow of a toy car, darting along the floor boards in the kitchen.

I don't like mice. I have nightmares in which they swarm around my feet and try to climb my legs. I wake up screaming. I could barely read Susanna Moody's *Roughing it in the Bush*—the passage about the mice crawling over her as she slept made me shudder.

Suze hates spiders. She's been dropping pennies into plastic bags filled with water and setting them around the cottage. She says the magnified coins look like eyes to the spiders so they won't spin their webs nearby—they don't like the feeling of being watched. Who does?

After making Natalie promise she will empty it when we catch the mouse, I set a trap in the kitchen using peanut butter as the bait.

We're sitting in candlelight in the living room after sunset. Music wafts from the CD player. It's a peaceful evening, the windows are open and crickets sing in the darkness.

Snap! I see the mousetrap jump about six inches into the air and fall to the floor with a thud. A dark lump is caught and it's not moving. Killed instantly, thank heavens.

"I'm not picking it up yet," Natalie says. "It's too fresh, let it sit." No one wants to touch a warm corpse.

We wait, the tranquil evening ruined by the small death on the kitchen floor. We can't get back to the meandering conversation we've been having for the last forty years or so.

Finally, Natalie flicks on the light in the kitchen and surveys the dead body. I watch from the safety of the living room.

Suze points at a glistening ball about a foot

away from the dead mouse. "What's that?" From where I sit, it looks like a red grape. Natalie bends closer to observe.

"Ew!" she screams. "It's a tick!"

I leap to my feet and start high stepping around the chimney. Suze rushes to me and grabs me by the arms squealing, "Ew, ew, ew!"

We don't know what to do. The engorged tick, which disengaged from its host at the moment of death, is so unexpected. We don't have a tick disposal plan.

The dead mouse is tiny in the trap. The tick is enormous—an alien—a Martian that emerged from a space ship.

Finally, Natalie gets the barbecue tongs. Gingerly, she lifts the mousetrap and crosses the kitchen floor while I watch, my body primed for an exit. She drops the dead mouse into the garbage and turns around for the tick. There's no way those barbecue tongs are going to safely transport that disgusting insect to its final resting place. She'll have to get closer. She takes up the broom and quickly sweeps up the tick. It rolls like a tiny armadillo into the dustpan.

Her footsteps are quick down the hall. I hear the toilet flush.

That night, I lie in my bed watching *Marcella*. Above me, I hear a golf ball rolling across the attic floor.

14
A MOUSE TALE

Kindergarten. We sat in a big circle on the floor. The teacher passed around a mouse. It was a very small mouse. It fit in the palm of thirty-one five-year-olds. Until it got to me. I didn't know that I was about to do what I was about to do. There was no prior thought or plan. I was sitting cross-legged, quietly, obediently as usual. And then, it was my turn. The mouse landed in my hand. Its little feet were scratchy. It twisted its tiny whiskered nose at me and blinked its small red eyes. And then its tail. It slithered across my fingers and I screamed.

It took a long time for the teacher and the janitor to locate the mouse. Everyone was mad at me for flinging it so far.

15
THUMP THUMP DRAG

I was sharing a cot with a cousin I'd only just met that afternoon. My sister Suze was in the bed on the other side of the room with a cousin she'd just met.

Our parents were still visiting in the living room. We could hear the drone of their voices, the rattle of the beer bottle case, our mothers' laughter.

The cousin in my bed, Julie, was a storyteller. And although her older sister lay in the bed across the room, Julie was the one holding the floor.

"When the woman got home, she opened the door of her car, and a bloody hook was dangling from the door handle."

I was not accustomed to younger sisters garnering all the attention. Julie was mesmerizing. Her stories were horrifying but I didn't want them to end.

She told the one about the couple parked in Lovers' Lane. The one about the man in the back seat at the gas station. And finally, she told Thump Thump Drag.

It seems a deranged prisoner had escaped from the lunatic asylum. Nearby, a mother and daughter were the only ones home at their house, their cottage actually, not unlike the one we were in right now. The mother hid the daughter in a closet upstairs and said, "Whatever you do, don't open the door!"

I pulled the covers up to my nose. Our room was dark. From across the room, I could hear Suze and my other cousin breathing.

The little girl in the closet, I could imagine her. Being locked behind a door was not beyond my experience.

The little daughter heard the sounds of a scuffle downstairs. She heard her mother screaming and some loud stabbing knifing sounds.

Then silence.

I held my breath. Julie grabbed my shoulder and I almost jumped out of my skin.

"Then the girl heard a sound coming up the stairs." Julie made her voice sound both hair-raising and husky. "Thump...Thump...Drag... That's all she heard. It was coming closer, thump, thump, drag."

I pictured the poor little girl, trapped in the closet, the knifed wielding maniac creeping down the hall toward her in ominous sound.

"Closer and closer, thump, thump, drag. Until finally, right outside the closet, she heard a big thump. And the little girl screamed and fainted."

Julie paused for effect. She let go the grasp on my shoulder and smoothed down the covers.

"When the little girl woke up, a policeman was carrying her down the stairs. She looked back toward the closet and saw her mom, lying on the floor. Both her legs had been chopped off."

There was a moment of silence in the room.

"Thump thump drag," Julie said, explaining the sound a body with no legs makes as it moves wordlessly toward a little girl locked in a closet.

From across the room Suze burst out laughing.

I laughed.

All the air I'd been holding in my chest flew out. I laughed and I laughed. But I didn't think it was funny.

16
WOODWORM

Why is it easier to remember the meanness of my childhood than the blandness? So often, I was bored. Lassoing the clothesline with a plastic skipping rope and galloping around the backyard. Wishing I was an outlaw. My tiny suburban heart beating in affinity with the gunslingers I'd seen on *Bonanza*.

My sister Suze dominated the scene. Insinuating everything I thought, did, and said was stupid. She was in my head, an insidious woodworm, chewing and gnawing and inhabiting me. I didn't know enough to doubt her. She was older. She'd been bigger than life for as long as I could remember. Overbearing. Smothering. Hovering. Lashing and defeating me.

Thinking back now, I wonder—why was she so preoccupied with me, or rather, with tormenting me? What wound her up like a deviant puppet-master fixated on tangling my life in a knot of confusion—preventing me from dancing, skipping, or walking on my own.

Our father. He may have been Suze's Geppetto. When she was a toddler, he still paid attention to his daughters. Family lore said he played with Natalie but he adored Suze, she was his prized pigeon.

I wonder now how my mother felt about that. I know what it's like when a lovely young daughter garners all the attention a man is capable of giving. It's a jealousy like none other — an invasive wormy envy for a girl who's done nothing to deserve it. I'd felt that way when Saffron was a teen. Sometimes I felt invisible. Was my mom able to hide her anger or did she redirect it into something less destructive like tightening up my loose pigtails or forcefully combing the knots out of my wet hair?

When I came along, four years after Suze, my father's interest in family life had evaporated. He'd switched to his passion for vodka. Suze noticed two things: there was a new baby in the house, and Daddy no longer had time for her. Guess who received Suze's wrath?

When I remember the years in the bungalow, I barely remember my parents or Natalie. I remember Suze. Her elbows and knees, her toothless mouth, her nasty tongue, and the whip, the lash, of the rider.

17
THE RIDING LESSON

I stop by Apple Acres to see if I can buy some decent strawberries. As my car crunches onto the graveled parking area, I'm launched back in time to the Freiderich's farm, the texture of the driveway, the slam of car doors—the sound of my mother, Suze and I arriving at the stable.

Suze, a velvet hard hat strapped to her head would hop onto a horse for her weekly riding lesson. Horses and riders walked slowly in a circle around the sawdust ring. The instructor, her fiery red hair loose and wavy to her shoulders, in a white turtleneck, jodhpurs, and tall black boots, stood in the center of the ring, a whip in her hand, giving instruction and smoking cigarettes.

I waited with my mom behind the observation window for an hour, an interminable weekly hour. The farm's owner, Mrs. Freidrich, collected horses and everything in the waiting room was a precious antique, rendered worthless in my estimation by the horse in its composition—there were horseshoe ashtrays, paintings of thoroughbreds, rearing Lipizzaners with clocks embedded in their stomachs, and horse brasses from old tack. But the piece that drew my attention over and over was Lady Godiva. She was solid black metal, smooth except for two raised nipples. Godiva and her mount, frozen in iron, bareback and bridleless.

I hated waiting but only slightly less than being left alone at home with my father. So, every week my mom dragged me along to Suze's riding lesson.

Sometimes, I dared myself to venture out of the observation room into the stable. My fear of horses confused me — other girls loved them. I kept daring myself to get over it.

The horses' names were tacked above their stalls. They stood with their giant round rumps to the aisle gazing out of small dirty barred windows. I watched their rear hooves that seemed poised to kick if I stepped too close.

The jet-black stallion, Perusso had a long unkempt mane. He stamped and snorted, pacing in his box stall. If I stood on a straw bale, I could look in through the bars, into the darkness, and sometimes catch Perusso's wild white eye.

My dread was that the horses would get loose, breaking through their tethers to gallop around inside the stable. I feared that once free their first mission would be to kill all the humans.

I was trapped there too. At the riding lesson. Not that those killer horses cared, but I was trapped there too.

18
BLACK FLAGS

1970. Tyler Walker died today.

I happen upon the line in an old diary.

I am going through my stacks of journals before shredding them, and the entry shocks me—jolts me back to that time when Tyler burnt up in the fish hut. He was a boy Suze and I had known from town. A bad boy, always in trouble. He'd broken into a fish hut out on the frozen lake, lit it on fire, and then couldn't escape. He'd died, so people said, trying to climb out through the chimney.

A few lines on in the journal, I'd reported Suze shouting, "Liar! I hate you!" when I'd told her the news.

Agony reverberates through the years.

I used to think there was a good reason for keeping a diary—now I can't remember what it is. Decades after, when all the pain is hidden and scarred-over, a single line still catches and mangles like a carelessly cast fish hook.

I ponder Suze's angry reaction—and all the millions of cuts and bruises inflicted on me, and by me, since.

The lake is calm. It's an offshore breeze. Something is floating near the corner of the neighbors' dock. At first, I think it's a beaver.

"What is that?"

Suze answers, "I don't know but it looks like a dead body, doesn't it? It's been out there all day."

I take the binoculars from their case and go out on the porch so I can get a better look. It's a Canada Goose, head down in the water.

As I pass by the fire pit on the lawn, I pick up the long bare stick we use to poke logs as they burn. I cross the beach, stepping carefully to avoid the piles of dark green goose shit. My shoes crunch over the deluge of zebra mussel shells that washed ashore this year after the die-off.

At the end of the dock, the goose's dark brown and white body floats like a feathered barrel. I look down into the water. The goose's long black neck disappears into the slimy underwater boards. It must have reached down to nibble something under the dock and got its head stuck. Misery rips through my chest.

The bird's wings are akimbo. The poor thing must have drowned, frantic and struggling to free its head from the boards. Its funny webbed feet float behind it like two black flags.

I reach the stick down into the water and with no effort at all push on the goose's neck. The head dislodges from the boards and floats up to the surface. One filmy black eye stares up at me.

The wind is from the south so the feathered corpse drifts out into the lake and away. I return to the cottage. The distress of the drowning leaving my body only slowly. Soon I will forget. Or not forget. But soon the desolation will float from my mind.

Suze crouches in front of the fireplace struggling to strike brittle matchsticks on the side of a damp matchbox.

19

WASPS

After a brief ignoble life of gnawing wood and working stiff-winged for his Queen, I guess he's going to die there, caught betwixt the reinforced screens in the door. A black wasp crawled in between two tightly drawn layers of mesh in the doorframe and now he's too dull or too exhausted or too frustrated to wiggle his brittle striped body out the way he came in.

Years ago, my father rigged up the double screen arrangement to prevent holes that invariably appeared from summer to summer — but insects get caught inside it and become petrified corpses. About six inches from this struggling wasp, lies the crackly black shell of one of his compatriots that must have climbed in and perished some years ago. Did this new wasp mistake him for a brother or a friend?

The smell of freshly mown grass and the sound of a cutter send me back to Tyler Walker pushing the old gas lawn mower, up and down the lawn, the toes of his shoes turning green by the end of the morning, my mother paying him $7.50.

I remember one day, Suze and Tyler were restless — running wild through the summer day. I was following them. We climbed the lattice up onto the cottage porch. Several wasps were busy on the wall, crawling, exploring, disappearing into a hole about the size of a fingertip.

Suze picked up a clothes peg and fit it into the hole where a wasp had just disappeared. Suddenly there was a swarm, a cloud of sizzling hovering wasps. Suze screamed and swatted at them. Tyler stood petrified and staring. I ran to the screen door and opened it. I don't know why I thought it was a good idea but I stood holding the door until Suze ran past me. She ran down the hall and out the back door onto the lawn. That's where my mom intercepted her. She must have heard the screaming. My mother pulled Suze's mohair sweater off over her head. There were wasps embedded in the sweater. My mom grabbed a can of Raid and started spraying. Suze was still bellowing.

For days after Suze lay on the couch in the darkened cottage. I visited. So did the doctor. Suze survived. The astronauts landed on the moon.

I'm not going to save this wasp as I might a spider or a moth. I won't stick a pen in and wiggle him free. I'm going to let him die that claustrophobic death. Trapped and pressed, disoriented and bitter.

It feels a little wrong but I know too well the piercing scorch of his stinger and I am finally realizing it was never something I did. It was always the wasp—all along, that venomous prick was something outside of me.

20
THE WEDDING PRESENT

For Suze's wedding present, I bought a set of colorful carved figures from Mexico. They were made of wood, their joints held together with metal pins. Some had dog heads or horse heads and others had heads of demons. Each had a chair, painted yellow, turquoise, or red. At least one of them had a hole in his fist so he could hold a tiny carved bottle labeled, *Mescal*. These figures were drinkers. They even had a tiny table. They were a fantastic sculpture — I thought she'd really love them.

Not long after her divorce, I'd ended up with the Mexican animal dudes. I kept them on a ledge, high above the sliding glass doors, way out of the reach of my tampering children. The sculpture sat up there against the dusty window catching cobwebs, the paint fading slightly in the western sun, the figures sat there, doing nothing.

Perhaps it wasn't a good wedding present after all. Perhaps art is in the eye of the beholder. Perhaps only good housekeepers should have sculptures in their homes.

My sisters and I have changed. The nights we drank tequila and sang our lungs out, dancing and hollering in western-themed bars—we packed up those memories long ago. Tonight we sit on the porch drinking tea and watching the sunset. The renters next door are noisy and partying. They have a dog and it's barking at nothing. When they drag a beer pong table out of their cottage, Natalie says, "Well. That's it. I'm going to bed." It's not even dark.

Suze and I follow her inside. I pour my tea down the drain.

21
GEESE AT NIGHT

It's past midnight and the geese are honking. Out on the dark lake they're flocking, complaining, or sounding an alarm. About what? Something.

I've never heard geese crying in the night before.

The rental cottage next door is occupied for the weekend by a group of men, they might be firefighters, it's hard to tell. They brought boats with them and were gone fishing all day but now in the darkness they're sitting around the fire pit, talking. One says, "There are no fucken fish in this lake." Another says, "Yeah, but are there supposed to be?"

I'm only awake this late because after the power outage (a transport truck crashed into a hydro pole in town) I need to spend time with my eyes glowing in the stream of my tablet-screen's light. I need a fix of electricity. Now, I wonder if these itchy tired eyes of mine will even close or if those geese will finally settle down and go to sleep tonight on the water — their legs dangling down into the cold dark lake.

22
LEAKING ROOF

It's been raining all year. It started drizzling during Donald Trump's inauguration and it's been raining ever since.

I'm sitting in the cottage living room listening to the roof leak. There's a steady beat in the kitchen ceiling and when I check in Natalie's room there's a line of drips pooling and falling from the strapping in the ceiling over her dresser.

It's hard to get anything done. I'm distracted. Running an anonymous Twitter account so I can follow and comment on political tirades—nervous that my phony account with three haphazard followers might get hacked and my real identity exposed.

I'm obsessed. I can't tear my attention away from the continuous "breaking" stories and "news flashes". The Trump story breaks and breaks and breaks like waves from an insane jet skier driving round and around in circles.

The roofers are scheduled for the first week in August. They're busy this year. All this rain. I wonder if I'll get anything done by then. I was planning to write a novel but I can't get started. I watch other people vacationing from the screened window. I can't enjoy the summer. I'm just gaining weight and reading Twitter. Wondering if the sun will ever come out again.

23
SEDORE STREET

Today, my cousin Hannah kayaked down the shore to the east, toward the point. On a dock, a young boy was frantically running around, yelling for help. In the lake at the end of the dock, Hannah could just make out a little face, sputtering for air — and two small hands waving just above the water.

She paddled hard toward the dock and then dove out of the kayak. In a few quick strokes, she reached the dock and scooped up the drowning boy. He wrapped himself around her like an octopus, sputtering, and crying.

There were three boys. One was the brother of the drowning boy. He'd been shouting and throwing things into the water to help. After Hannah set the drowning boy safely onto the dock, a third boy, with yellow hair, jumped into the water. "I'm not drowning. See?"

The yellow-haired boy felt it important to show Hannah that the water at the side of the dock wasn't over *his* head.

Hannah demanded the boys take her to their parents. She marched them up the street, one sopping wet child, Hannah in her bare feet and soaking workout clothes, the brother who told everyone they passed, "My brother almost drowned-ed!", and the yellow-haired boy.

Sedore Street runs south from the lake to the centre of town and is lined with old cottages that are gradually being converted into year-round homes with double garages. Hedges flourish. There are no sidewalks. Lawns are dotted with wooden wishing wells and plastic spinning zinnias in beds of goldenrod. Radio music rocks from screen windows. Cheap lawn chairs sit askew on front stoops.

At the top of the street, the boys turned into a yard. Hannah knocked on the door. The boys' mother answered. "What have they done now?" Evidently, she was house cleaning. Her ponytail bounced on top of her head and yellow rubber gloves dripped water on the doorstep.

Hannah explained that if she hadn't been kayaking, at that precise moment, it would be a very different story. The mother yelled at the boys, "I told you not to go down to the lake!"

After dinner I take Hannah's two daughters to the ice cream store. I wait, holding a dripping chocolate mess for Mercy, the youngest, to buckle up her seatbelt. I reverse carefully from the busy parking lot under the flapping plastic flags — you never know when a kid might come darting out of nowhere toward the pink cartoon cut-out ice cream signs and the Muskoka chairs and picnic tables.

There's construction on the main street. I drive slowly as we bump over plates in the road and crevices. The girls are quiet, slurping their ice cream. We turn toward the cottage. On the sidewalk, a boy on a scooter kicks desperately to keep up with a yellow-haired boy on a tiny bicycle. The yellow-haired kid jumps the curb and rides out directly in front of me. Pedaling hard, he meanders and weaves — showing off down the road, taking for granted that I'll slow down for him. We follow carefully behind.

"Look at that dumb kid," Mercy observes between licks.

I'm looking. He swerves down Sedore Street. I'm looking. I grew up in this town. I know who that yellow-haired kid is and who he will become.

24
TRASH TALK

My sister Suze was beautiful. Model beautiful. Tall. I could almost see her boney knees and elbows transforming into something desirable except I knew they were her weapons.

Eye shadow, blue, straightened hair. She coated her skin with film from a pot and brushed blush onto her cheekbones. She blinked her eyes, mascara drying, in a plastic makeup mirror. One light bulb flickering.

I can barely repeat what our mother said. She was only trying to protect us, to keep us safe.

"You're beautiful just as you are," she meant. Instead, she said to Suze, "You look like a slut."

25
BUCKTHORN

Here's the story Suze tells me while we're sitting on the back deck of our mother's house at happy hour. That's the afternoon interval before dinner when Suze and my mother drain a bottle of Rosé—happy hour.

"See that tree?" She motions at a nondescript tree, with leaves—a deciduous tree among the pine and spruce and fir. "That tree," she says, "Gets covered in little red berries. But they don't ripen. They take so long. Not even in October. They're finally ripe. So then, the leaves fall off and you can see the berries." She uses her hands. "Red red, all over the tree. And the Robins come. They must be Northern Robins, because they haven't migrated and it's October. The robins come and eat all the berries, which have fermented in the tree and the robins get drunk, and then they drop down into the birdbath and splash around like drunken idiots."

Suze tells me this because her deck chair is facing the Buckthorn. It's directly in her view, and what else is there to talk about?

This is what I have to look forward to when she and I move here for the winter.

At the edge of the garden, a hummingbird

hovers by the Bee Balm. It finally feels like summer. There's a long time to go before fall.

26
SQUIRRELS IN THE ATTIC

"Do you want to take a look?" John Joiner is blocking the hallway with his stepladder, the panel in the ceiling pushed back.

The attic. The vast dark space above the cottage. Home to a thousand bats and a hundred years of smuts and fusties. I don't want to look at anything in particular but I have a strong desire to feast my eyes on the sweep of space under the dormers. Sometimes, I fantasize about nailing down floorboards, installing solar panels, and renovating the attic into an immense lakeside studio. While John Joiner steadies it with his hand, one foot on the bottom rung, I climb up the wooden ladder.

My eyes adjust and I look around in the darkness. Everywhere, I see pin pricks of light, a tiny milky way in the old rotted roof. That explains why it's been leaking so badly.

Broken black walnut shells and shiny brown chestnuts cover the attic floor. Ohhh — so it wasn't golf balls I'd heard rolling around up here.

"That's no mouse, you got there," John Joiner calls up to me. "It's a squirrel."

And this is its nut storage.

John's plan is to repair all the gaps and holes where a squirrel could get in before he deals with the creature itself.

The next morning, while my sisters and I are still in our pajamas drinking coffee, John Joiner comes back with a live trap.

"It's humane," he tells us. "It's called Have-a-Heart."

He disappears once again, up into the hole in the ceiling with the trap. He will capture the squirrel, and then let it go outside to continue its existence in a tree nook, or wherever it is that squirrels live. John Joiner comes and goes all day and I hear him sawing and hammering, his careful footsteps moving back and forth along the rafters.

We're out all the next day. The bookstore in Uxbridge has received the book of poems I ordered and my sisters and I eat a nice lunch at The Mill. On the way home, we stop at a market in a farmer's field and buy berries and fresh brown eggs. Just before sunset, John Joiner returns.

"Heard anything up there?" he asks. We shake our heads, no. The truth is I'd forgotten all about the squirrel in the attic.

"I'll go up and have a look," John Joiner says. "Once he's trapped, we've only got 24 hours to get him out of there."

I hadn't thought about the poor little squirrel in the humane trap, thirsty and confused, possibly calling out to his squirrel family and friends, help, help, I'm trapped.

After a few minutes, John Joiner steps down out of the attic onto the ladder carrying the trap.

"Did we get him?"

"Yup."

John climbs all the way down and turns the trap so we can see inside. A plump red squirrel lies in rigor mortis on the bottom of the trap, its tiny paws curled — its eyes open wide in fright.

"I set the trap up on a ledge but it was on the floor when I found it. Must have been flailing around so much he knocked the whole kit'n'kaboodle onto the floor."

We contemplate the squirrel's last minutes.

"So more of a Have-a-Heart-Attack trap," Suze observes.

I feel bad. All that hard work to gather those chestnuts and now they'll all go to waste.

John Joiner takes the trap and the squirrel with him when he goes, leaving us his invoice on the kitchen table.

27
OLD COOKBOOK

I get out the old cookbook my husband and I used to use. I mean, the cookbook I used to use. He'd just eat all the fantastic food I made—enjoying it more heartily than was required. His appetite was always one of his more appealing features.

Lately I've been dreaming dreams with him in them. We're reconciled, or we're considering it, and I wonder if it's because time has created a distance that allows memory to forget. When I wake up, I'm disturbed, and embarrassed, and grateful that no one can read my mind. Or can they? I mean, can he?

These days I'm cooking for my sisters and myself. We're living a quiet, calm existence—the screened windows open to the breeze and the lake noise, the motor boats and the deliriously happy children playing in the water on a hot summer's day. The fan on the ceiling turns and the floor model oscillates, south to west to northwest and back. No radio. No music. No newspapers. No guests. No pets. We reuse our plastic bags several times and they're often set to dry on the knobs of the kitchen chairs.

I'm making chicken kabobs in Indonesian marinade with peanut sauce. I wonder if he remembers this dish, one of my favorites. I'm not bothering with skewers. Too much fuss. I just heat the cast iron frying pan to a sizzle and fast fry the chunks of chicken breast. I considered lighting the barbecue. I thought about my ex-husband lighting the barbecue and standing out there in the late afternoon sun, sweating and downing a quickly warming lager, and then another, and then another.

I thought about it and felt a little sad. Somehow, I conspired this aloneness for myself even though solitude was never something I pursued.

I'm glad my ex is not here. I'm glad I'll eat my dinner with my sisters and they'll remark on how good it tastes. I'm glad I'll go to bed alone, early, before the sun has finished setting. I'll watch the sky turn pink outside my window and the night sounds will begin — the crickets, and the motorcycles, and the waves lapping at the shore.

I'll watch some movie of my own choosing on my tiny tablet, balanced against a cushion on my stomach. And I'll go to sleep, at peace, looking forward to nothing really. Just moving at a pace that keeps me alive and hoping I stop dreaming dreams with him in them.

28
HERON

My friend Alice and I are having lunch, overlooking the river in Uxbridge, when, like a kite, a flash of white sails beneath the branches, wings spread like the pattern on a Japanese kimono. It's breathtaking, a heron from above — this must be God's view.

Alice isn't aware of how flat she is today. The minutes of silence that pass between us are like being underwater — I'm holding my breath. The absences, where her laughter used to ripple, are like photographs of a ghost.

The heron alights beyond our view and begins to wade slowly down the river toward us. The waitress sets down our bill and says, "Take your time, ladies."

I snap photos of the heron as it strolls deliberately on its long cane legs through the shallow river, head cocked, fishing.

It's hot. We've been shopping. Alice bought very little. She seems unable to be kind to herself today. Her imagination has disappeared. Nothing appeals.

I place some silky plastic Canadian money on the tray and Alice adds coins.

The heron climbs the bank and disappears

into the tall grass.

I'm waiting for Alice near a life-size statue of Humphrey Bogart, checking my phone, when the waitress approaches holding the little black plastic tray.

"Did you ladies pay your bill?" Her tone cannot be mistaken for anything other than snarky. I stare at the four Toonies on the little tray.

Where are the green $20 and the purple $10 I put down? I picture my money sailing down from the deck into the river.

I'm confused. Embarrassed. Afraid. I would never leave a restaurant without paying. How dare this waitress accuse me. Is she accusing? What if the money is gone? What if she's *pretending* the money is gone?

Then I remember. Alice said she was going to pay with her credit card and leave the tip in cash. But she's in the bathroom.

Alice emerges from the darkness of the restaurant. Weary and defeated. Life has knocked her around the last few years like a marionette in a child's hand.

"Do I pay here?" she asks the waitress.

As we leave, I wonder if $8 was enough of a tip.

On the glass door, I read a sign, PULL, and I tug on the brass rail. The door doesn't budge. Alice reaches past me and pushes the door to open it.

Maybe I have been doing that lately, reading all the signs backward.

29
THE STILL SMALL VOICE

I've been waiting for a boom. A grand pronouncement. A voice that rattles my bones from the outside.

I pray for direction. For strength. For courage. For guidance. And my muted heartbeat answers pitter, patter, pit.

From my window, I see the stillness of the lakeside. The trees silent. Beads of rain dropping one by one by one from the pine needles. The lake is quiet. The waves, a gentle pulse on the shore of small stones.

Listening for an answer, I realize, I've been hearing it all along. It's been here in my calm decisions. In the easy movement of each day. Hearing the answer like a shallow breath, a gentle thought. Life's consent, a whispering wave. The still small voice of Awe.

30
SESQUICENTENNIAL

My little cousin, Mercy comes into the cottage carrying a flat piece of wood, cut into the shape of a fish. She tells me it's for the Paint-A-Perch contest the town is running in celebration of the Sesquicentennial.

She seems tired. Exhausted by her life as an eight-year-old. It's been too cold and rainy this summer. Normally, she'd spend all day in a bathing suit running around the property with her sister, playing on the beach, and begging adults, like me, to accompany her to the sandbar where the water is shallow and the lake bottom sandy. But not this year.

She asks if I can help her paint the fish plank, so I get out some watercolors and pastels. I envision a watery blue, blotchy fish — with maybe a yellow eye. I'm enthused by the project — delighted that Mercy is participating.

Mercy lays her head on her arm and looks at the blank fish canvas and the paintbrushes I've set out. Her long dark hair covers most of her face. She seems disenchanted.

I have to go. My sisters and I are driving around the lake today to Minesing for a quilt show at the Simcoe County Museum. We leave

Mercy at the kitchen table, dipping a reluctant paintbrush into a jar of water.

Traffic is light and for a change, the sky is clear. No rain clouds in sight today. I turn on the GPS and program it to avoid the big highway. In a little over an hour, we have meandered our way around Cook's Bay and up to the city on the northwest corner of the lake.

The parking lot of the museum is packed full of cars baking in the sun. I squint into the brightness and slam the car door shut. The heat of the day presses down. It's the second or third day for this kind of weather. Back at the cottage, Mercy has probably gone swimming.

Inside the museum, my sisters are greeted by their quilter friends and disappear into the cavernous room housing the quilt show. I decide to save the quilts until the end. It won't take me long to survey them. Sure, they're beautiful and oh-so-much-work, these pieced geometric combinations of fabric scraps, but they're bedspreads after all. Blankets assembled by all these middle-aged women with short gray hair. Women like my sisters, and me.

I wander down the hall into the museum to look at the exhibits. The first is a longhouse. It looks rather skimpy but I'm curious to know what it feels like inside. There are plastic coals in a fire pit in the middle of the floor. Wolf pelts hang from the ceiling and the benches along the walls have animal hides strewn on them. The roof is covered loosely with bark. It feels poorly constructed and the sensation I was seeking does not materialize.

Farther along in the gallery I encounter a buckskin-clad female figure with knee-high moccasins and a fringed skirt. A braided headband encircles her wig of shiny black hair. The figure is bending forward toward a tree stump upon which she is presumably preparing one of the three sisters: corn, beans, and squash. The exhibit is aimed at schoolchildren. Kids about the age of Mercy.

I meet Natalie and Suze outside at lunchtime. It's a beautiful day. Mature pine trees tower all around creating a high green ceiling and dappled shade from the midsummer sun. We sit at a picnic table and eat hotdogs and pie. The soundlessness of the forest floor, the quiet hush created by the cathedral of trees stirs my pioneer blood. I look around at the little church and its neighboring schoolhouse. The sensation of olden days shimmies through my veins.

After lunch, my sisters and I wander through the outdoor exhibits. Our ancestral past feels close. The items on display are familiar—all our lives we've been surrounded with this old Canadiana in our cottage and pump house. We could open a museum ourselves.

Under the trees, a woman pedals an ingenious circular knitting machine like a bicycle, creating marvelous wool socks. Nearby, a blacksmith pokes at an open fire, pulling out glowing red rods, hammering them before a small audience of middle-aged husbands.

The blacksmith has laid out a collection of iron items — knives and locks and keys. I point out to Natalie that her husband might like one of the black bottom frying pans for his campsite.

The blacksmith picks up a long axe-shaped tool and asks Natalie if she knows what it is. She plays along — unlike me, she likes interactions with strangers.

"The traders knew there was only one thing the Indians loved more than war," he tells Natalie with confidence. "And that was smoking." He waves the metal axe. "So they invented these Tomahawk/Peace Pipes — the Indians loved these things! Couldn't resist them."

I avert my eyes and look down at the black metal tools spread out along the bench. Natalie is quiet for a moment, listening politely. Then she cocks her head to the side and asks the blacksmith, "Do you mind a little feedback on your presentation?"

"Oh, this isn't a presentation," he protests.

"I'm just talking."

Natalie clears her throat. "Right, I know, and I don't mean to criticize. I just want to point something out." I know what's coming and my heart speeds up a beat or two. "When you say, the Indians loved war as much as smoking, that's not really true."

The blacksmith waves away her remark like a pesky housefly. "That's not me saying that. That's in the books. The history books."

Natalie's voice rises to match the blacksmith's volume. She says, "The books are wrong too."

A small crowd has gathered. The man beside Suze shuffles his feet in the pine needles. "Most Natives weren't warlike—they were peaceful," Natalie continues. "And they certainly weren't any more violent than the colonists who brought the guns and gunpowder!"

The blacksmith talks over my sister, mansplaining and defending his understanding of the metal tools used by the settlers in their trade with the First Nations people.

Nevertheless, she persists. A few in the crowd nod and murmur their assent with Natalie. The blacksmith is outnumbered. He stops talking. Natalie has made her point. I'm proud of her.

As we walk away, a man asks the

blacksmith where he gets his raw materials and the blacksmith launches into an explanation of anchor chains.

Before we leave the museum, I walk through the quilt show. The entries for the "Canada 150" category hang in the hallway. My eyes dart over the blocks of red and white, the maps of Canada, the Mounties and stitched Tim Hortons cups. One whimsically pieced quilt captures my attention. Separated by russet maple leaves are appliquéd blocks — a pair of hockey skates, an inuksuk, and a wind-blown pine tree growing out of rock. I vote for it as best in show.

Mercy has left the art supplies and her painted perch on the kitchen table. On it, she's painted a brown house with a strip of green grass and a yellow sun in the sky. Peculiar choice for a fish, I think. Later, she tells me it's supposed to be the gazebo in the town parkette but she hates it. It didn't turn out the way she imagined it in her mind's eye.

I tuck the perch into the box behind the fireplace. No sense letting a good piece of kindling go to waste.

31
SOLAR ECLIPSE

On the day of the solar eclipse I sit on the back deck of Mom's house, nowhere near the sun or the sky, firmly planted on the freshly stained cedar deck, reading *The Pied Piper* by Nevil Shute. My mother's garden is a study in the color green, every tree is a different shade, a different hue, and every movement of wind or bird fractures the green into another nuance, deeper or brighter, darker or paler, jade, lime, asparagus, forest, moss, olive, mint.

The chipmunk that lives under the deck discovers that I have left a few nuts and seeds on the metal leaf sculpture at the back of the garden. A pair of blue jays try to scare away the chipmunk but it ignores their flashing blue wings and shrill calls.

Mom tells me that Stephen Leacock was friends with my Great-Great-Uncle Burkholder. That he used to visit when he was in town and bury his bottle of beer in the cool dark earth behind the cottage. It was always shady back there, I remember.

The beer story is ironic because Uncle Burk's wife and her sister, my Great-Grandmother, were members of the Women's Christian Temperance Union and they disapproved of beer, buried or not.

Sitting at Mom's house, a few miles from the cottage, enjoying the shade, I think about Stephen Leacock and his *Sunshine Sketches*. I wonder if that's what I've been doing this summer, writing sketches—except my stories feel so dark.

The eclipse passes, unnoticed by me.

I try to talk Mom into going over to the cottage for a swim. Today is hot enough—how summer ought to be. But she resists, preferring to sit and watch the garden.

The birdsong this afternoon is constant and distracting. I can barely read a paragraph before I have to look up to see if I can identify the singer. The birds, shrouded in the branches, hide their brilliant whistles, and when they soar over to the birdbath to splash around, I'm surprised that they're just ordinary birds—robins and starlings and wrens. A tiny yellow banana of a finch perches on the mesh feeder choosing all the nyjer seeds. A hummingbird zizzes from Bee Balm blossom to Bee Balm blossom bypassing the glorious daylilies with their wide open pink throats.

I'm hot. I miss the lake. Miss the blue in my eyes. I turn another page of the novel. I don't notice time is passing.

32
LIKE A DRAGONFLY

Passion? I've given up on it. Or has it given up on me? Maybe I'm living it. Maybe all my saying, *Sure!* has resulted in a passionless passion.

I believe. I believe in my stuff and in my work and in my lifelines. They fill my day. My days are full of passions—or what were my passions before I possessed them.

Maybe, passion is the longing. When something is so hard to reach, when it's unmanifest, and then when you're holding it in your hand it's just light like a dragonfly. No burden, no heaviness, just a lifting up and a landing.

33
THANKSGIVING

On Thanksgiving Day, the turkey goes into the oven around ten o'clock in the morning. My sisters and I expect a crowd for dinner — our mom, our children, Natalie's husband, some of our cousins, and a few friends.

October has been unseasonably warm and the rain that plagued us in June and July is long gone. Natalie and I go for a walk before the family arrives.

"Ew!" A dead squirrel lies prone against the sidewalk. There's been a bumper crop of roadkill this year — raccoons, skunks, porcupines. They get hit by cars as they try to navigate their way from the bush and undergrowth to open lawns and the promise of walnuts and chestnuts and acorns from the trees surrounding the cottages, and the smoldering and smelly green compost bins left beside cottage doorsteps and sheds.

The lake is calm and reflective. A paddle-boarder glides by. The trees along the shore have only just begun to change color. A smattering of crimson and yellow leaves wave in the slight breeze. The cedars are loaded with clusters of rusty cones.

On the lake, the Canada geese continue to

congregate. Dozens of them float about, mingling and communing in their comical honking language. Every now and then, they take flight with a flapping frenzy, swooping and swirling out over the lake, returning to settle further down the shore. Groups of small white seagulls compete for gathering space along the beaches. I find it hard to accept that the summer is over but the fact of the bird migration is everywhere. Soon, my sisters and I will close up the cottage, pack up the food and empty the crumbs out of the toaster. We'll haul in the porch furniture, and call the plumber to turn off the water. But as long as the weather is mild like this, I have no plans to leave, and neither do my sisters.

The kitchen fills with the smell of roasting turkey. Pies and people begin to arrive. The fridge door opens and closes a dozen times, as snacks are prepared and bottles stowed.

Today, Natalie has taken it upon herself to keep the kitchen tidy. That's her contribution to the meal. She dislikes cooking, so she declares herself the dishwasher for the day and as the tea and coffee cups mount and various dishes are prepared she hovers near the sink ready to wash off utensils and dry pots and pans before they take up space on the counter.

Suze is making the gravy. I'm on potatoes and vegetables. The turkey emerges from the oven mid-afternoon, a beautiful orange color, a crisp crackling skin. Suze hauls it from the pan and sets it on a large platter to rest before Natalie's husband carves it.

Suze sets the large roasting pan back on the stove so it straddles two elements. As the dark gooey grease on the bottom begins to bubble, she sprinkles in flour, stirring and scraping at the drippings with a wire whisk. She lifts the lids off the pots of Brussels sprouts and mashed potatoes on the back of the warm stovetop. "Where did the guts go?"

"The what?"

"The gizzards. The neck, the heart. The stuff that came out of the turkey?"

Natalie answers, "In the fridge. Did you want them for the gravy?"

"No." Suze crosses to the fridge and pulls open the door. "Just the water they were cooked in."

She scans the shelves for the pot of gizzard brew.

"Oh." Natalie looks confused, then contrite. "I dumped out the water."

Suze and I stare at her. I wonder for a moment about her sanity. Suze is more generous. "That's okay, I'll use the Brussels sprout water."

Natalie says, "I dumped that out too."

We light candles and crowd around two tables pushed together. No one is listening to anyone else. We all just eat, pass the cranberries, and make merry. Cousin Hannah, hoisting a wineglass, declares she is thankful for family this year. No one follows suit, except to murmur agreement with her gratitude—good food, good friends, good wine, or so the sentiment goes. Glasses clink. The food is delicious, the gravy a little bland and pale, but no one mentions it.

After dinner, I take another walk along the shore. The early evening air is suddenly crisp and clear and the sky turns an astonishing tangerine orange.

On a wide expanse of lawn, I spy a red fox. She is standing with her mangy white-tipped tail sticking out behind, her jaw snapping like a stapler as she eats something in the grass. I glance down—the dead black squirrel that we saw earlier is gone from beside the road.

I watch the fox eating her Thanksgiving dinner for a few minutes. I feel grateful for the time I've spent at the cottage this year. Grateful for the wildlife. The life and death and life. Grateful for my sisters, and my cousins, and my mom. Grateful for the lake and the sky. Grateful for my solitude and this sojourn. Grateful and at peace. Finally, grateful and at peace. I wish the fox a goodnight and walk back to the cottage in the dusk.

~The End~

ABOUT THE AUTHOR

Sandy Day is the author
of *Fred's Funeral* and *Chatterbox Poems*.
She is a graduate of Glendon College,
York University where she studied
English Literature and Creative Writing
under Michael Ondaatje and bp nichol.
Sandy is a facilitator for the
Toronto Writers Collective.

Sandy lives in Georgina, Ontario, Canada.

Read new work
and join Sandy's Mailing List
at www.sandyday.ca

Follow
Facebook.com/SandyDayWriter/
Twitter @sandeetweets
Instagram @sandeesnaps